The Hide-and-Scare BEAR

To all at Brisley Primary School,
for showing everyone the kind way to play
and much, much more – I.B.

A BRUBAKER, FORD & FRIENDS BOOK,
an imprint of The Templar Company Limited

First published in the UK simultaneously in hardback
and paperback in 2015 by Templar Publishing,
Deepdene Lodge, Deepdene Avenue,
Dorking, Surrey, RH5 4AT, UK

www.templarco.co.uk

ISBN 978-1-78370-135-3 (hardback)

ISBN 978-1-78370-189-6 (paperback)

Printed in China

The
Hide-and-Scare
BEAR

by Ivan Bates

B F & F

BRUBAKER, FORD & FRIENDS

AN IMPRINT OF THE TEMPLAR COMPANY LIMITED

There once
lived a bear who
was not very good –
didn't think about
others or behave
as he should.

He picked his nose;

he gobbled his food.

Not a "please"
or a "thank you" –
he was horribly rude!

But the worst
thing of all,
this mischievous bear
liked playing a game
he called "Hide and Scare".

He would
creep up
and then,
on the count
of three...

jump out with a

ROAR!

from behind
a tall tree.

"Hide and Scare,"
growled the bear,
"is such marvellous fun!"
And he laughed and he laughed
as he watched them all run.

The animals
decided enough
was enough.
Owl called a meeting:
"We need to get tough!"

"This bear
must be stopped,
it's our duty to try.
All those in favour
stand up and say 'Aye!'"
"Aye!" cried the animals,
getting enthused.
"Nose!" squeaked Mouse,
who was very confused.

"What we need," declared Owl,
"is a friend without fear.
So who will step forth
as our brave volunteer?"

There was a long silence…

...then a quiet voice said,
"I can help, not with anger,
but with kindness instead."

Standing alone,
with a twitchy pink nose
stood a soft little rabbit
who then said, "I propose..."

"That maybe this bear's
not as bad as you say.
He's just never been shown
the kind way to play.
What he needs, I believe,
is some gentle advice –
a short rabbit lesson
on how to be nice."

"Nonsense!"
scoffed Badger.

"You're mad!"
Squirrel squeaked.

"Preposterous!"
laughed Fox.

Then...

ROAR!

They all shrieked!

The animals ran
as fast as they could,
except for brave Rabbit;
there she still stood!

Now the Hide-and-Scare Bear
hadn't known this before,
so he snarled and he growled
and he roared even more!

But no matter how
loudly he stamped
or he growled,

or how deeply he snarled,
or how wildly he howled –

Rabbit still
DID NOT MOVE!

Sad and exhausted,
Bear finally stopped,
and with a sigh
and a whimper,
slumped down
on a rock.

"If you're finished,"
said Rabbit,
"*I've* something to tell.
A little more kindness
would suit you
quite well!

A wave and 'Hello!'
is the way you should greet,
not a snarl and a growl
and a stamp of your feet.

Say a 'How do you do?',
give a shake of the paw.
Or a smile and a bow,
if you want to do more."

"But for those who are special,
just one thing is right.
Hold open your arms and…

HUG…THEM…TIGHT!"

And then,

something

AMAZING

happened...

Bear said,
"Thank you, dear Rabbit,
you've helped me to see
how wonderful kindness
and cuddles can be.
From this moment on,
I'll be changing my ways.
I'll be giving out hugs
for the rest of my days!"

Do you know what?
That bear *was* good,
and from that day on,
hugged as much as he could.

With a "How do you do?"
and an "If you please",

he gave
all his new friends
a Big Bear squeeze!

Which
everybody
loved...

...most of the time!